Dear Parent:

Congratulations! Your child is taking the first steps on an exciting journey. The destination? Independent reading!

STEP INTO READING® will help your child get there. The program offers five steps to reading success. Each step includes fun stories and colorful art. There are also Step into Reading Sticker Books, Step into Reading Math Readers, Step into Reading Write-In Readers, Step into Reading Phonics Readers, and Step into Reading Phonics First Steps! Boxed Sets—a complete literacy program with something for every child.

Learning to Read, Step by Step!

Ready to Read   Preschool–Kindergarten
• big type and easy words • rhyme and rhythm • picture clues
For children who know the alphabet and are eager to begin reading.

Reading with Help   Preschool–Grade 1
• basic vocabulary • short sentences • simple stories
For children who recognize familiar words and sound out new words with help.

Reading on Your Own   Grades 1–3
• engaging characters • easy-to-follow plots • popular topics
For children who are ready to read on their own.

Reading Paragraphs   Grades 2–3
• challenging vocabulary • short paragraphs • exciting stories
For newly independent readers who read simple sentences with confidence.

Ready for Chapters   Grades 2–4
• chapters • longer paragraphs • full-color art
For children who want to take the plunge into chapter books but still like colorful pictures.

STEP INTO READING® is designed to give every child a successful reading experience. The grade levels are only guides. Children can progress through the steps at their own speed, developing confidence in their reading, no matter what their grade.

Remember, a lifetime love of reading starts with a single step!

Copyright © 2009 Disney Enterprises, Inc. All rights reserved. Published in the United States by Random House Children's Books, a division of Random House, Inc., 1745 Broadway, New York, NY 10019, and in Canada by Random House of Canada Limited, Toronto, in conjunction with Disney Enterprises, Inc.

Visit us on the Web!
www.stepintoreading.com
www.randomhouse.com/kids

Educators and librarians, for a variety of teaching tools, visit us at
www.randomhouse.com/teachers

Library of Congress Cataloging-in-Publication Data
Redbank, Tennant.
Pixie Hollow paint day / by Tennant Redbank ; illustrated by the Disney Storybook Artists.
   p. cm.—(Step into reading. Step 4 book)
Summary: Art-talent fairy Bess asks her fairy friends to come to a party and help make more paint so that she can finish her new painting.
ISBN 978-0-7364-2580-3 (trade pbk.) — ISBN 978-0-7364-8067-3 (lib. bdg.)
   [1. Fairies—Fiction. 2. Paint—Fiction. 3. Artists—Fiction.] I. Disney Storybook Artists. II. Title. PZ7.R24455Pix 2009
[E]—dc22
2008023708

Printed in the United States of America   10 9 8 7 6 5 4 3   First Edition

DISNEY fairies

Pixie Hollow Paint Day

By Tennant Redbank

Illustrated by the Disney Storybook Artists

Random House 🏠 New York

Bess was an art-talent fairy. She was working on an important painting. She had been painting day and night for almost two weeks. It hadn't been easy. She was having trouble getting the picture just right. But now she was almost done.

Bess held a bottle up to the light. It looked empty. She turned it upside down. A single drop of blue paint slid out.

"Oh, polka dots! I'm out of blue paint!" she wailed.

Bess thought for a minute.

She grabbed a tube of purple paint.

She squeezed it flat. Only a tiny bit

came out.

"Oh, no! I'm out of purple, too!" Bess

groaned. She needed to get more.

Bess went over to her paint shelf. There was no blue or purple paint. The red paint was almost gone. She'd left the lid off the yellow paint and it had dried up. And the only green paint she had was lime green.

Bess put her hands on her hips. There was just one thing to do. "It's time for a paint party!" she declared.

Making paint by herself was a lonely task. But making paint with other fairies was fun!

Bess sent invitations to her friends.
She asked Tinker Bell, Rani, Beck,
Fawn, Lily, Prilla, Silvermist, Fira,
and Rosetta. None of them were
art-talent fairies. Still, everyone said
yes—everyone except Rosetta.

When she got the invitation, Rosetta
went to see Bess. "Paint making?" Rosetta
said. "That sounds messy." She didn't like
getting dirty!

Bess shrugged. She had plenty
of help.

Bright and early on a sunny morning, the fairies gathered in the meadow.

"Reporting for paint duty!" Tink said. She gave Bess a little salute. "Point me to the paint pots!"

Bess laughed. "Not yet," she said.
"First we have to find some colors."
Bess told her friends that paint was
made from plants and flowers and other
things found in nature. The fairies
could find what they needed all over
Pixie Hollow.

Bess had made a list for each fairy.
It told them what to look for.

The fairies were eager to begin. Lily knew right away where to find the buttercups and sunflowers for the yellow paint—in her own garden! She picked a huge armful of both.

Tink flew into the forest. She was
looking for pine needles. They made the
best dark green paint.

Prilla picked a patch of violets.
They would make a lovely shade of
purple paint.

Rani filled an entire basket with
raspberries and cherries. Bess could use
them to make the perfect red paint.

Silvermist was in charge of the orange paint. She carefully dusted the wings of an orange butterfly. A little butterfly dust went a long way!

Blueberries were great for blue paint.
And Fawn and Beck knew of a huge
blueberry bush where their bird friends
always went to eat.

White paint came from chalky
pebbles deep in caves. Bess sent Fira to
find those. The light-talent fairy used
her glow to light the way.

Meanwhile, Bess set up a row of coconut shells in the meadow.

One by one, the fairies came back with their finds.

"Put the blueberries in that shell over there," Bess told Fawn and Beck.

"What lovely violets!" Bess said
to Prilla.

"Those sunflowers and buttercups
will make such bright paint!" she gushed
to Lily.

Each fairy put what she had found into one of the coconut shells. Bess added some linseed oil to each shell. This would help turn each item into paint. Then the fairies stepped into the shells and started to stomp!

Fawn stomped on the blueberries. "Oooh, the berry mash is oozing into my shoes!" Fawn cried.

"You should try the pine needles," Tink said. "They tickle my feet!" She lifted up a pine-green foot to show everyone.

"This is hard! I want to eat the raspberries," Rani said. "They smell so good!"

Fira was working on the white paint. She smashed the pebbles with Tink's hammer. Then she mixed the bits with the linseed oil.

Kindhearted Lily couldn't bear to crush her sunflowers and buttercups. She turned them over to Prilla. Lily worked on the purple paint instead.

"You are all doing such a great job!" Bess said. "This is going to help me so much with my painting!"

The fairies kept stomping and crushing and mixing and churning. Their feet were all sorts of bright colors. And they were having a good time.

"Tell us about your painting, Bess," Silvermist said.

Bess thought for a moment. "Well, it's a big picture of the Home Tree in late-afternoon sunshine. The painting has a golden glow." She paused. "I like it, but something's missing."

Bess had an idea. "I know!" she said. "I'll show you my painting! Maybe you can help!" She flew out of the meadow.

A few minutes later, Bess was back.
In her hands was a large painting. She
leaned it against a tall flower stem.

The fairies crowded around to look at Bess's painting. It was very pretty. But Bess was right. Something was missing.

"Maybe some of this new paint will help," Prilla said. She always looked on the bright side.

"Maybe," Bess said. Then she sighed and gave her friends a smile. "I know what I want to do. I don't want to work on this painting right now. Let's put away all this beautiful paint!"

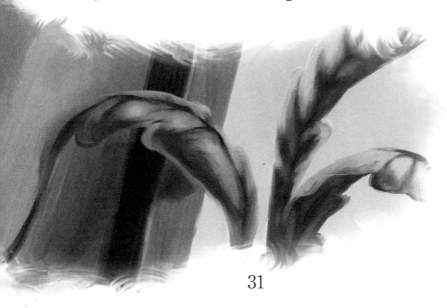

The fairies quickly began to bottle the paint. All of a sudden, they heard a noise. It came from just outside the meadow.

"What was that?" Tink asked. The fairies heard twigs cracking. They heard leaves crunching. They heard . . . *RIBBET!*

A giant frog leaped into the clearing!

"Strongjump!" Fawn cried.

Strongjump was Fawn's frog friend.

He heard her call and launched himself at her.

"Strongjump, no!" Fawn shouted.

It was too late. Strongjump landed right in the coconut cup of red paint. It splattered all over!

From there he made another mighty leap—straight into the green paint. *Splash!* Green paint sprayed the meadow.

"Wait, Strongjump!" Fawn yelled.

But Strongjump didn't want to wait. He hopped into the orange paint and the white paint and the blue paint. He overturned the purple paint. He knocked over the yellow paint.

Paint splattered everywhere!

Fawn flew right up to Strongjump.
She came nose to nose with him. "Stop!"
she yelled. He stopped.

"Good frog," Fawn said. She patted
him on the head.

"It's my fault," Fawn said to the other fairies. "I told Strongjump I would play with him today. Then I forgot. He came looking for me. He was so happy to see me that he didn't watch where he was going."

"That's okay," Bess said. "A little paint never hurt anyone!"

The fairies looked at themselves. A little paint? Hardly! They were covered head to toe with every color.

Prilla giggled. There was paint in their hair. Paint on their clothes. Their legs were colored up to their knees. And they had paint on their cheeks, noses, elbows, and ears.

The other fairies began to smile. They put their arms around each other. Then they laughed until their sides hurt.

Then something caught Lily's eye. "Oh, Bess!" she cried. "Your painting!"

The fairies all turned to look at Bess's painting. It had been splashed with paint, too! Streaks of red and orange and green and yellow crossed the canvas. White spots and blue splotches dotted the Home Tree. A big blob of purple filled one corner.

Bess flew over to the painting. She
was very quiet. The other fairies watched
her. They didn't know what to say.

Bess looked at the painting up close.
Then she backed up and looked at it
from far away. She studied it from the
left and from the right.

Slowly, a smile spread across her face. She turned around.

"I like it!" she told her fairy friends. "I really like it! This is just what it needed!"

Then Bess hugged Strongjump. "What a perfect paint day! I knew we would end up with lots of paint. But I never thought we'd fix my new painting, too!"